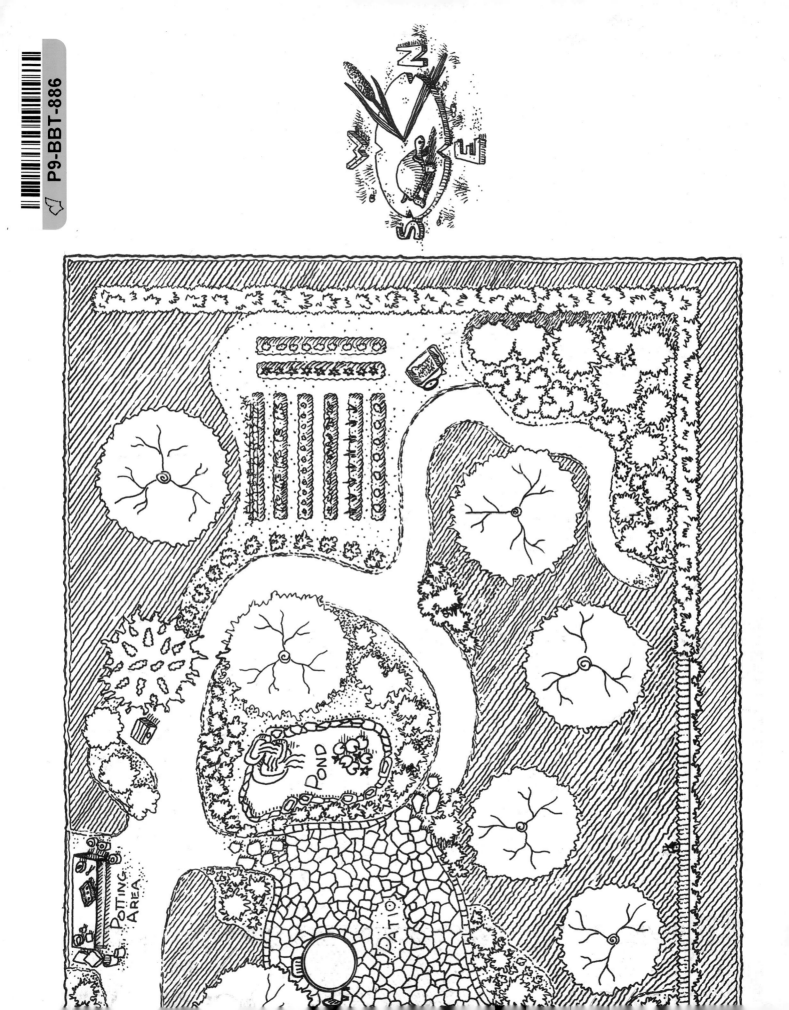

For Mary Kay

Layout and Design:
Jose Barcita – Barcita & Barcita, Incorporated, Chesapeake, Virginia
www.barcita.com

Consulting Editor:
Cindy Huffman – Advertising Concepts & Copy, Virginia Beach, Virginia

Legal Counsel:
Mimi Glenn, Esquire – Williams Mullen, PC, Virginia Beach, Virginia
www.williamsmullen.com

Web & eBook Design:
Donna Conversano – JeanAlan Design, Inc., Norfolk, Virginia
www.jeanalan.com

The text is set in 18/20 point, Mrs. Eaves Roman, Italic & Bold.
The illustrations were created using acrylic dyes and prismacolor pencils.

Library of Congress Control Number: 2004093550

ISBN 0-9754342-0-9 Hardcopy

First Impression

To order additional copies or for instructions on how to have your book personalized by the author and/or the illustrator,
please visit our website at www.rubyleethebumblebee.com

Bumble Bee
PUBLISHING
A Division of Bumble Bee Productions, Inc.
www.bumblebeepublishing.com

Proudly published, printed and manufactured in the United States of America.

RUBY LEE A Bee's Bit of Wisdom BEE the BUMBLE BEE

Story by Dawn Matheson
Pictures by Pamela Barcita

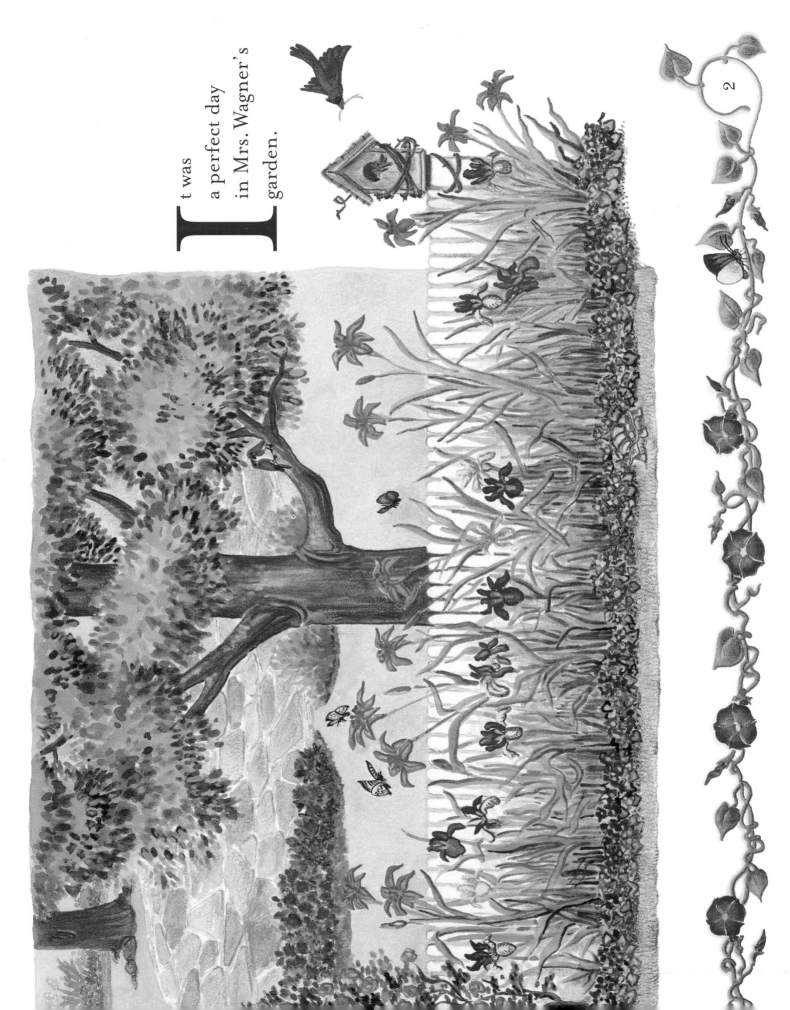

It was a perfect day in Mrs. Wagner's garden.

2

The garden was dazzling in its new spring colors.

Under a clear sky of robin's-egg blue, the trees wore leaves of fresh emerald green, and flowers bloomed in every color of the rainbow.

LIFE BEGAN in a GARDEN

Ashley lived next door to Mrs. Wagner and often stopped by to visit. The two had become great friends.

Most Saturdays you could find them sipping raspberry tea on the patio as they watched their furry, feathered and buzzing friends take delight in the garden.

Mrs. Wagner said the garden was their playground.

The bunnies tumbled through the clover and played hide-and-seek under the periwinkle.

The squirrels leapt from tree to tree, impressing Mrs. Wagner and Ashley with their athletic prowess.

The birds sang beautiful cantatas as they cheerfully played in the fountain. Ashley and Mrs. Wagner couldn't help but smile.

Ashley especially enjoyed the bumble bees. She found it remarkable how they tirelessly danced from flower to flower collecting pollen and nectar.

Mrs. Wagner said they were God's most industrious creatures.

7

After tea, Mrs. Wagner asked Ashley if she would pot some flowers to decorate the patio.

"I don't know!" Ashley said with a gasp. "I-I don't think I can. I mean, your garden is so beautiful. I could never make something so pretty. And what if I ruin the flowers?"

"Oh honey, that's just silly," said Mrs. Wagner. "Of course you can do it. You've helped me so many times, I'm sure you know just what to do.

"Now, I have a few chores to take care of inside. I'll be back to check on you in a while."

With that, Mrs. Wagner picked up the tea set and went into the house, leaving Ashley with the pots and flowers.

Although Ashley usually knew what to do, now that she was alone she doubted her memory. How much dirt should she use in each pot? How hard was she supposed to pack it down? How deep should she set each flower?

Oh, why hadn't she paid more attention? She wanted to cry out of frustration. "I'll just make a mess of it. I'm no good at anything!"

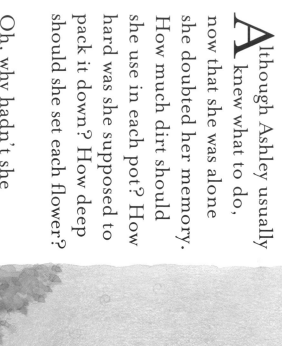

"Tsk, tsk," she heard a sweet voice say.

Turning, she hoped to find Mrs. Wagner coming to relieve her from this impossible task.

But Mrs. Wagner was nowhere around.

"Who's there?" Ashley cried out.

"Calm down," said the voice. "I'm over here."

"Where?" asked Ashley. "I don't see anyone."

"Over here on the butterfly bush," the voice answered.

Ashley moved closer to the flowering shrub and inspected it closely. There she saw a bumble bee.

"Good morning!" said the bee.

Ashley had to sit down to keep from falling over in shock. "A bee. I'm chatting with a bee," she said in disbelief.

"Exactly!" said the bee. "But not just any bee — I'm a bumble bee!"

"I don't mean to be rude, Miss Ashley, but I couldn't help overhearing your dilemma."

13

"I've seen you in the garden many times. I know Mrs. Wagner wouldn't ask you to do anything you're not capable of."

Still in shock, Ashley somehow managed to remember her manners, and she asked the bee its name.

"I'm Ruby Lee. Ruby Lee the Bumble Bee!"

Ashley looked closely at Ruby Lee. She was a beautiful specimen.

Dressed in fuzzy yellow and black, her little round body seemed huge under its dainty silver wings.

Her big, bee eyes were bright and friendly, and her cheeks were ruby-red — like her name. Her smile was as sweet as honey.

Just looking at her made Ashley feel better, and for a time she forgot she was speaking with a bumble bee.

"Now, Miss Ashley, is there any reason you couldn't pot those flowers for Mrs. Wagner?" Ruby Lee asked.

"Well", said Ashley, "I'm not good at anything. What if I break a pot? What if I ruin her beautiful flowers? What if —"

"Enough!" said Ruby Lee.

"Life is full of challenges. It's up to us to turn every challenge into an opportunity. We bees learn this very early on."

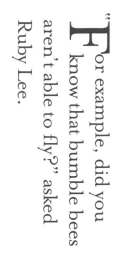

"For example, did you know that bumble bees aren't able to fly?" asked Ruby Lee.

"What do you mean?" asked Ashley with a puzzled look.

"I know you can fly — I've seen you!"

"Well, of course we do fly, but technically we're not supposed to be able to," explained the bee.

"Huh?" responded Ashley.

"Scientifically speaking, our bodies are far too big for our little wings. We shouldn't be able to fly."

"That's amazing," said Ashley.

"Yes, it is," agreed Ruby Lee.

Flight of the Bumble Bee

lift/weight ratio

0 1 2 3 4 5 6 7 8

$\sqrt{\frac{L}{W}} \frac{x/ws}{y^2}$

wind speed (kph)

HEIGHT 2cm

SIZE NEEDED FOR FLIGHT 1cm x 3cm

1cm

·5

Wing length 1cm

LENGTH 3cm

WEIGHT 288m

Conclusion: Bumble Bees cannot fly.

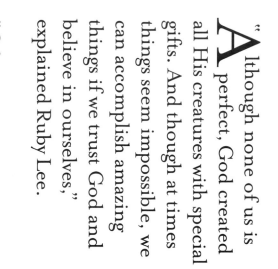

"Although none of us is perfect, God created all His creatures with special gifts. And though at times things seem impossible, we can accomplish amazing things if we trust God and believe in ourselves," explained Ruby Lee.

"Of course you can pot those flowers for Mrs. Wagner. You are a talented and bright young lady! I'll sit here with you while you work," said Ashley's tiny new friend.

After pondering the wise words of Ruby Lee the Bumble Bee, Ashley was inspired. She scooped potting soil into each pot, then selected the flowers she thought prettiest.

As she set each plant on top of the soil, she held it gently so the roots wouldn't be damaged.

Gradually, she remembered everything that Mrs. Wagner had shown her.

S he and Ruby Lee had a wonderful time chatting while Ashley worked.

With each pot, Ashley gained more confidence.

In the end, only one pot suffered a minor chip, and the flowers were beautiful!

"Well done!" exclaimed Ruby Lee. "Well done."

Ashley couldn't help but smile. Her heart was filled with pride.

She had done it!

At that moment, Mrs. Wagner returned to the garden. "Oh Ashley, what a wonderful job! I knew you could do it."

As Mrs. Wagner and Ashley arranged the pots around the patio, Ruby Lee hovered close by.

"Mrs. Wagner?" asked Ashley. "Did you know that bumble bees aren't able to fly?"

"Well yes, Ashley, I do know that. My mother told me the story many years ago, when I was just about your age.

"She said that when God made the bumble bee, it shouldn't have been able to fly, but God whispered in its ear, 'You can do it.'

"The bee trusted Him, and so it flew."

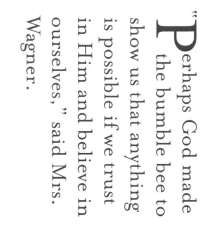

"Perhaps God made the bumble bee to show us that anything is possible if we trust in Him and believe in ourselves," said Mrs. Wagner.

At that moment, Ruby Lee flew to Ashley's shoulder and whispered in her ear, "bee–lieve!"

And with that, the wise little bee flew off into the garden, doing a few loop-the-loops.

Just because she could.

Glossary

Butterfly Bush	A bush with clusters of red, purple and white flowers that attract butterflies
Cantata	A musical piece that's sung by one or more voices (*kun-TAHT-uh*)
Capable	Able to do something (*CAPE-uh-bull*)
Challenge	A problem that really tests your abilities (*CHALL-inj*) — the "a" rhymes with pal
Confidence	The belief that you can do something (*KAHN-fuh-denss*)
Dazzling	Shining brilliantly (*DAZZ-ling*)
Dilemma	A situation in which none of your choices seems good (*dih-LEM-muh*)
Disbelief	Not believing what your eyes or ears are telling you (*diss-bee-LEAF*)
Forget-Me-Not	A delicate, five-petaled flower that grows in many parts of the world. Ruby Lee is sitting atop a Forget-Me-Not on the cover of this book.
Frustration	A feeling of defeat or the feeling that you can't accomplish something (*fruss-STRAY-shun*)
Gasp	To draw your breath in quickly, usually because of a shock or surprise. (*GASSP*)
Impressing	Having a good effect on or causing someone to form a good opinion of you (*im-PRESS-ing*)
Industrious	Hardworking (*in-DUST-ree-iss*)
Inspect	To look over carefully (*in-SPEKT*)

Nectar	A liquid given off by flowers that is used by bees to make honey *(NECK-ter)*
Opportunity	A chance to improve yourself or a situation *(ah-poor-TOON-i-ty)*
Periwinkle	A plant with white or blue flowers that have square edges *(PEAR-y-wink-uhl)*
Pollen	A fine dust in flowers that sticks to your fingers and leaves a yellow stain *(PAH-lin)*
Pondering	Thinking something over *(POND-er-ing)*
Pride	The good feeling you get after doing something well
Prowess	Ability *(PROW-iss)*
Puzzled	Not sure of something *(PUZZ-uld)*
Relieve	To free someone from an unpleasant task *(ree-LEAVE)*
Remarkable	Amazing, in a good sense *(ree-MARK-uh-bull)*
Responded	Answered *(ree-SPON-did)*
Scientifically	Doing something by the rules of science *(sigh-en-TIFF-ik-lee)*
Specimen	A sample or example of something *(SPEH-sih-min)*
Technically	According to science or proven rules *(TEK-nick-lee)*
Tirelessly	Without getting tired *(TIRE-less-lee)*
Tsk	A sound you may make when you don't agree with someone

Inspirational Notes

This story is dedicated to the remarkable Mary Kay Ash (1918–2001). She was a woman of great faith and uncompromising values and has been an inspiration to so many people.

Born into a family of modest means, Mary Kay overcame personal loss and many professional challenges to become one of the world's most respected women.

Through her uncomplicated formula for success of putting God first, family second and career third, she became a phenomenon in the business world.

Among her credits are the National Business Hall of Fame, *Fortune* magazine's Businesswoman of the Century, Lifetime Television's America's 25 Most Influential Women, *The World Almanac*, and the Horatio Alger Distinguished American Citizen Award.

The bumble bee was her mascot. She always wore a bumble bee pin on her lapel.

The character of Mrs. Wagner was created after Mary Kay's mother, who told her daughter from a young age, "You can do it!"

Ruby Lee, the wise little bumble bee, is named after another remarkable woman, Rubye Lee-Mills, a friend to Mary Kay and an inspiration in her own right.

In the illustrations you'll see an old wooden box labeled "Stanley Home Products" — the name of the company where Mary Kay began her business career.

On the book's cover, Ruby Lee is sitting on a Forget-Me-Not. The flower was chosen by illustrator Pamela Barcita because she hopes young readers will always remember the wisdom imparted by this endearing and whimsical title character.

Mary Kay facts provided by Mary Kay Autobiography, by Mary Kay Ash, ISBN 0-06-092601-5, 1981, and The Mary Kay Tribute Website at www.marykaytribute.com

Lessons From Ruby Lee the Bumble Bee

Page 7

A challenge can often make us feel anxious. It's normal to be anxious or even afraid.

We must try even when we don't feel confident about our abilities.

Page 8

We can all help build confidence by encouraging those around us, "Of course you can do it!"

Parents, notice that Mrs. Wagner left Ashley alone with the challenge. Many times we feel compelled to "take over" when our children feel challenged because we don't want them to be stressed. It's a natural tendency, but instead we should allow our children the opportunity to grow.

Page 9

Ashley's self-defeating attitude can be a lesson for all of us. In the wise words of Mary Kay: "If you think you can – you can. If you think you can't – you're right!"

Page 14

It's important that, even when we're under extreme stress, we remember our manners and are courteous to others.

Page 16

We have to be wary of getting caught up in the "what if" web. It serves no purpose.

It's up to us to turn every challenge into an opportunity.

Page 19

Although we're all imperfect creatures, we have special gifts. If we trust in God and believe in ourselves, we can accomplish amazing things.

Notice how Ruby Lee builds Ashley's confidence: "Of course you can pot those flowers for Mrs. Wagner. You are a talented and bright young lady!" Mary Kay always taught that we should praise people to success.

Page 20

Notice how Ashley listens to Ruby Lee's story. So many times, we miss important bits of wisdom because we're not paying attention.

Although Ashley is uncertain of her abilities, she works through the fear to accept the challenge. This is a clear example of courage.

Page 21

Even when Ashley chips one of the pots, she doesn't let a little "road-block" set her back. She perseveres until the challenge is completely met.

Page 22

Accepting and completing a challenge is very rewarding.

Be proud of your accomplishments.

When others acknowledge your accomplishments, accept the praise willingly and be humble.

Notes of Gratitude from Dawn

God has blessed me so many times in my life. I hope this book glorifies Him.

The list of others to whom I will be eternally grateful:

My incredibly talented sister, Roxanne Rask, as this book would not have been possible without her contributions and support. Thanks, Roxy!

My remarkable 11-year-old niece, Katie Rask, for her valuable input and direction. Watch for her on the bestseller lists! LUB U Bug!

To Wayne Barr for his encouragement and creative direction. I'll never, never, never forget you!

THE MOST INCREDIBLY TALENTED creative team on the planet, Pam, José and Cindy! I am so blessed to have found you, and I am honored to have had this opportunity to collaborate with you. You guys are awesome!

And finally, to my loving husband, who supported me through this endeavor. Thank you for always bee-lieving in me, honey!

Bios

Dawn Matheson is a new and refreshing author committed to creating quality books for children. She is a member of the Society of Children's Book Writers and Illustrators.

In addition to writing, Dawn loves traveling, gourmet cooking, and spending time with her family. She lives in Chesapeake, Virginia, with the love of her life, Scott Matheson, and their two feline children, Sassy and TJ. She has 20 nieces, nephews and godchildren.

Award-winning designer/illustrator *Pamela Barcita* has won numerous awards, including an Athena. She was honored by the Society of Illustrators in Los Angeles. A member of the Society of Children's Book Writers and Illustrators, she has illustrated over 20 children's books, including the popular *Boots the Cat* series. In addition, Pamela has illustrated coloring books and authored *African Wildlife, A Photographic Journal. Ruby Lee the Bumble Bee* reflects Pamela's love of the outdoors. An art teacher at the college level, Pamela lives in rural Chesapeake, Virginia, with her family, four cats, and two cockatiels. She and her husband formed Barcita & Barcita, Incorporated, in 1988.

Veteran designer *José Barcita* has worked at some of Virginia's most prestigious advertising agencies and garnered numerous advertising and design awards in local, national, and international competition. A co-founder of the The Society of Communicating Arts, he is a recipient of the Silver Medal Award, which was established by the American Advertising Federation to recognize individuals for their creative excellence, outstanding contributions to advertising, and social responsibility. José has two children and five grandchildren.

Cindy Huffman is an award-winning freelance writer and editor who lives in Virginia Beach, Virginia. She has worked at one of Virginia's largest advertising agencies and written for national and international clients. Cindy is a past president of the The Society of Communicating Arts. Her father authored numerous children's stories, so she was delighted to collaborate on *Ruby Lee the Bumble Bee.* She has one cat, a feisty Siamese.

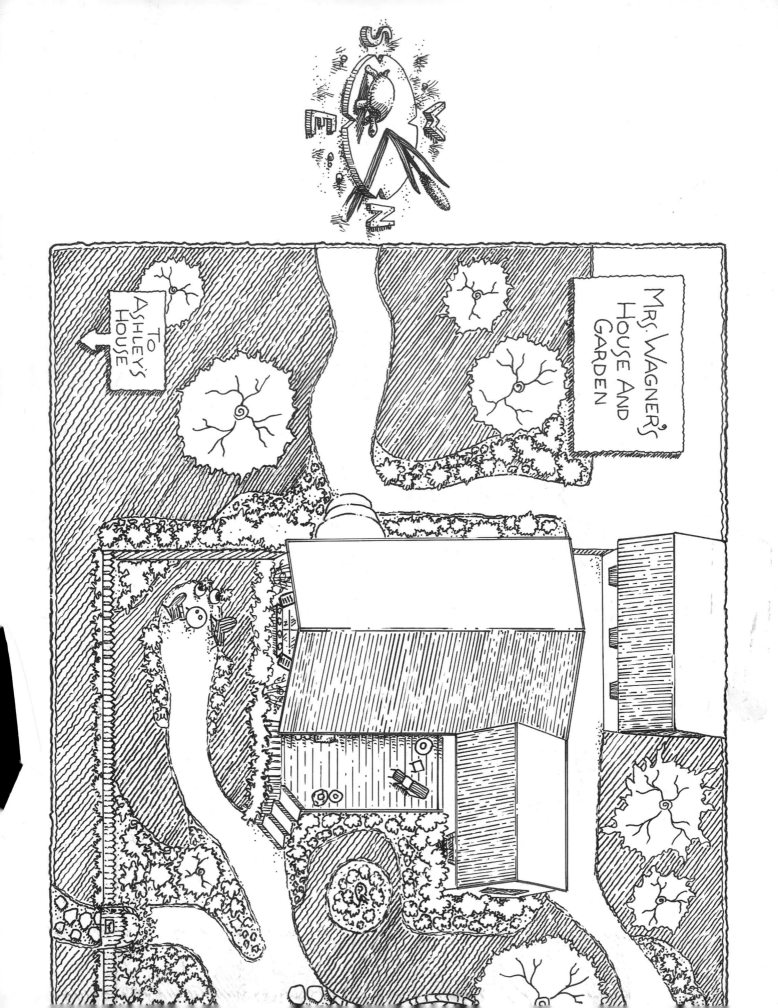